SPOOKY DAVE'S
SNAPPER BITES BACK

SUNNYSIDE
PRIMARY SCHOOL

Collins
RED
STORYBOOK

First published in Great Britain
by CollinsChildren'sBooks in 1995
1 3 5 7 9 8 6 4 2

CollinsChildren's Books is a division of HarperCollins*Publishers*
Ltd, 77-85 Fulham Palace Road, London W6 8JB

Printed and bound in Great Britain
by HarperCollins Manufacturing Ltd, Glasgow

0 00 674898 8

SNAPPER BITES BACK

by Karen Wallace
Illustrated by Judy Brown

CollinsChildren'sBooks
An Imprint of HarperCollinsPublishers

TO CASSANDRA

Chapter One

Clever Trevor yawned and climbed down from his high chair beside the swimming pool. It was a hard life being a lifeguard. All day he had to flex his muscles and look tough. Then he had to get down from his chair and walk round and round the edge of the pool. It was a rolling, bow-legged walk, a bit like a cowboy who has been sitting on a saddle all week. It was how all tough lifeguards were supposed to walk and it had taken him a long time to learn.

Clever Trevor sighed. The truth was it didn't matter what he did. Nobody seemed to notice how tough and handsome he really was. Nobody, that is, except his friend Bulging Brian.

Bulging Brian was also a lifeguard. He was tough and handsome and he had forearms like joints of boiling bacon. He also had a head the size of a hard-boiled egg. Bulging Brian was about as smart as a hard-boiled egg, too.

"Saved anyone recently?" asked Bulging Brian as the two of them were changing after a long, hard day by the pool.

"Nah," said Clever Trevor. "Too busy."

Bulging Brian nodded knowingly. "By the time you've decided which dive to do—"

"Yeah," said Clever Trevor. "It's usually too late."

"Yeah," agreed Bulging Brian as he pulled on his tight leopard-skin trousers and his 'Hunks Have It All' sweat-shirt. "Got any plans for this evening?"

Clever Trevor looked in the mirror. He was deeply tanned as if he had just come back from holiday. The tube of Top to Toe Tan Treatment had said: Use as needed.

Clever Trevor smirked to himself. He had needed the whole lot.

"Same as usual," he replied.

Bulging Brian grinned. "You mean, go home. Get dressed. Go out and show off."

"Yeah."

Clever Trevor and Bulging Brian pushed through the revolving doors on to the street. Neither of them noticed the little old lady who went flying out the other side.

"See ya at the club then," said Bulging Brian as he slicked back his gluey blonde hair.

Clever Trevor climbed into his buttercup-yellow sports car and revved the engine so loudly, a baby in a pushchair began to howl. Then he roared off down the street, shaking leaves from the trees and frightening little old ladies as they pruned roses in their front gardens.

There was a pile of letters waiting when he got home. Actually, they were mostly brochures and special offers. Clever Trevor filled out all the coupons he could find because he liked to have lots of envelopes to open. It made him feel popular. Sometimes, if the envelopes were easy to open, he would stick them down again so that if he didn't get a lot of letters the next day, he could always open the old ones again.

At any rate, it wasn't often that he got a proper letter so Clever Trevor was surprised to find himself looking at a plain white envelope with his name typewritten on the front. Not only that, the name on the front was his real name, Trevor Prat, which was a secret to be kept from as many people as possible.

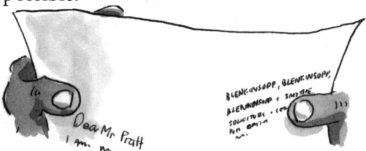

Clever Trevor read the letter. Then he read it again. Then he made himself a cup of tea with five teaspoons of sugar and half a tin of evaporated milk. Then he sat down and read the letter again.

His Great Aunt Emily had died and left him Molehills, the farm she had lived in all her life.

At first Clever Trevor was astounded. He had never known his aunt very well. But after a while, he began to get used to the idea. In fact, he rather fancied owning lots of land and not doing much.

"So you're going to be a farmer," said Bulging Brian as the two of them sat at the bar of *Nerds*, their favourite nightclub. "Um, what exactly does a farmer do?"

Clever Trevor sucked at something red and fizzy through a long straw. "They drink tea and watch television, mostly," he said. He blew a few bubbles and stared into his glass in a moody, movie-star way. "And sometimes, in the middle of the night, they have to get up and, ah, milk the chickens."

"Wow," said Bulging Brian, looking at his friend in a completely new light. "That's amazing."

Chapter Two

As the buttercup-yellow sports car
lurched down the muddy track to
Molehills Farm, Clever Trevor tried to
recall what he remembered about his
Great Aunt Emily.

All he could think of was a
bristly little woman,
who sucked a pipe
and always wore
trousers and had
a terrier called
Snapper who
never left her
side. Once,
when Clever
Trevor was six,
Great Aunt
Emily had sent
him a toy farm with
real hay and bits of
wood cut up into tiny
logs. But he hadn't like the
smell so his mother had taken
it away and given him a
Batman costume instead.

The sports car plunged into a deep puddle, spraying mud all over the windscreen. Clever Trevor flicked on the wipers. Suddenly he was in the middle of a farmyard, staring at a large brick house with the words Molehills Farm written in black letters on top of the front gate.

Clever Trevor got out of the car, strolled towards the house with his rolling cowboy walk, slipped and fell flat on his face in the greasy mud that covered the yard. There was a snort of laughter behind him.

"I'm terribly sorry," said a girl wearing gumboots and a muddy overall. "I didn't mean to laugh. You just looked so funny."

Clever Trevor glared at her. He wasn't supposed to look funny. He was supposed to look tough and handsome.

"Who are you?" he asked rudely as he clambered to his feet.

"I'm Nellie Bucket," said the girl. "I've been looking after your aunt's farm." She paused. "I've been expecting you."

Clever Trevor stared at her. She wore glasses and a bobble hat and didn't seem to have any lipstick on. He had never seen a girl wearing a bobble hat before. And he had never spoken to one who didn't wear lipstick.

"Well, you don't have to bother any more," he said, wiping the mud out of his eyes. "I know all about farming."

Nellie Bucket gave him a strange look. "But I thought you were a–" She blushed. "There's just the milking to do," she said quickly, and she put down the pitchfork she had been carrying and walked away across the yard.

Clever Trevor looked beyond her to a group of chickens in the orchard. They were pecking grass and seemed perfectly happy. They didn't look as if they needed milking.

He walked up the path and opened the front door.

A picture of Great Aunt Emily was hanging in front of him. In one hand she held her terrier, Snapper. The other hand rested on a long knobbly stick.

Clever Trevor looked at his great aunt's face. Then he looked at the terrier. The two of them were almost identical, except that his aunt looked a bit fiercer.

A fire was burning in the sitting room and a pot of tea and biscuits had been laid out on a table in front of the television. That's more like it, thought Clever Trevor, not stopping to wonder who had done it for him.

He gazed around the room. There were pictures on the wall, the sofa and chairs looked comfortable and in front of the fire was a handmade rug with a picture of a terrier woven into the middle. Above the fire… Ugh!

What on earth is that? thought Clever Trevor, and he leant forward to get a better look. There must be some mistake, he thought. That bossy girl must have put it there as a joke.

Above the fire, in pride of place, was a
battered metal dish with a name
engraved on it.

Ugh! Ugh! It was a dog bowl!
Clever Trevor puffed himself up to his
full height and even though no one was
watching, he stuck out his square jaw
and looked tough.

"I'm not having a dog bowl in my
sitting room," he muttered. He opened
the window, threw out the bowl and
watched as it skidded across the yard
and landed underneath a rosebush.

Grrrr!

It was a low, menacing sound.

Grrrr! Grrrr!

Clever Trevor spun round. It sounded just like…

Brrrrrmmm! Brrrrrmmm! There was a squeal of tyres in the yard and mud splattered all over the window. Bulging Brian jumped off his bike and shambled across the yard.

"Watch out for the–" yelled Clever Trevor, but he was too late.

Bugling Brian skidded on the mud and slid on his nose right up to the gate.

As Clever Trevor turned to leave the room, he looked up at the bare wall where the dog bowl had been. It would be a good place to hang that big picture of himself in his pink and green swimming trunks with all his life-saving medals hung round his neck.

"Funny that noise, though." Clever Trevor shrugged. Must have been the central heating pipes, he thought, wisely. Old pipes make all sorts of strange sounds. He'd heard about it on a video somewhere. But as Clever Trevor walked down the hall to open the front door, a peculiar thought occurred to him: he hadn't seen any radiators in the house.

Chapter Three

That night Clever Trevor slept badly.
In the next-door room, Bulging Brian
snorted like a tethered bull and every
time he turned in his sleep the
floorboards shook. But it wasn't the
snoring or the shaking floorboards that
kept Clever Trevor awake. It was the
sound of a dog yapping and howling.

It was a strange, hollow sound. Sometimes it seemed to be coming from far away and sometimes it sounded as if it was coming from the hall.

Three times Clever Trevor went downstairs, and each time the yapping stopped when he reached the bottom step. Worst of all, every time he went back to his room, rain was pouring on to his bed because the window had mysteriously blown open.

After the third time, his bed was as wet as a sponge and he went to sleep in an armchair.

"Best sleep I've had for ages," said Bulging Brian the next morning, rubbing his eyes and yawning like a hippopotamus. He slapped thick slices of margarine on his bread, smeared lumps of peanut butter over the top and covered the lot in a snowstorm of sugar.

"Didn't you hear that dog yapping?" asked Clever Trevor. He was standing in the doorway in a filthy temper. His brand new white trainers were covered in mud and he had ripped his shiny yellow track suit on a rusty nail.

"Dog?" said Bulging Brian. "What dog? I didn't think there was a dog here."

"Nor did I," muttered Clever Trevor as he pulled bits of straw out of his hair and dropped them on the floor.

"Why are you wearing straw in your hair?" asked Bulging Brian through a mouthful of sugar and peanut butter.

"I'm not wearing straw," muttered Clever Trevor. "I was in the barn giving the cows their corn." He paused and looked superior. "You wouldn't understand."

As he spoke he remembered the surprised look on the cows' faces as he had scattered the corn on the ground. They hadn't seemed to understand either.

"Gosh," said Bulging Brian, looking impressed. He slurped his tea like a camel at a water trough. "What about the sheep?"

"Oh, they're scratching for worms and building nests right now," said Clever Trevor in a knowing way. "It's better not to disturb them."

Bulging Brian looked puzzled. "That's funny," he said. "I've got a picture book that says–"

Clever Trevor glared at him. "I don't need a picture book to tell me how to run my farm," he snapped, pouring tea into one of Great Aunt Emily's china cups. Then through the kitchen door, he caught sight of the portrait. The stream of tea overflowed into the saucer, ran over the table and poured on to the floor.

Great Aunt Emily's face had changed.
Snapper's face had changed.
Great Aunt Emily was scowling.
Snapper was showing his teeth and
looked as if he was growling.

Bulging Brian stood up and pulled on
his black and yellow leather biking
jacket. Then he wiped his mouth with a
tea towel. "Better get back and startle a
few swimmers," he said, sticking out his
chest and flexing his muscles. "Now

you're a farmer, you don't have to worry about all that."

"You're right," said Clever Trevor, still staring at the painting. "I don't have to worry about anything, anymore."

As he spoke, an idea occurred to him and a completely different look crossed his face. It was a worrying sight. Bulging Brian was about to ask if he'd hurt himself when Clever Trevor said, "Will you help me move that painting? I want to put it somewhere else. Like on top of the rubbish dump."

Bulging Brian looked at the portrait of Great Aunt Emily. "Do you think you ought to?" he asked slowly. "I mean, it was her farm after all."

Clever Trevor stuck out his lower lip and thrust his square jaw into the air. He looked tougher than ever before. "It's my farm now," he said. "I can do what I like."

Bulging Brian thought about this. Something still didn't seem right but he wasn't sure what. "Yeah," he said finally.

So Bulging Brian lifted and pulled and Clever Trevor gasped and tugged. Nothing happened. The painting of Great Aunt Emily wouldn't budge.

It was as if it was fixed to the wall
with concrete.

"Tell you what," said Bulging Brian as he climbed on to his motorbike. "Why don't you get someone to come and paint over the top of it? The other day, I saw a man drawing terrific pictures on the pavement outside the swimming pool."

Clever Trevor remembered the pictures. They were full of palm trees, golden beaches, turquoise seas and girls in bikinis wearing lipstick. "That's a good idea," he said. "Send him out tomorrow." He walked back to the house as Bulging Brian roared out of the yard like a two-ton bumblebee. Inside, the colour of Great Aunt Emily's face seemed to have changed. It was purple.

Then Clever Trevor noticed something that made his mouth drop open and his knees knock. Snapper had disappeared from the painting!

Clever Trevor didn't stop to comb his hair or change his clothes. He jumped straight into the buttercup-yellow sports car.

"You're working too hard," he told himself, as the car bounced down the muddy track. "You need a break."

Five minutes later, as he walked through the door of the *Skipping Pig Inn,* Clever Trevor had convinced himself that he had imagined everything.

Chapter Four

Henry and Hilda Bucket had owned
The Skipping Pig for many years. They
had known Great Aunt Emily well and
it was their only daughter Nellie who
had been helping out at Molehills Farm.

At first they were pleased to see
Clever Trevor.

"You sit yourself down," said Hilda
Bucket, who was large and friendly and
made an elephant seem like a cuddly
toy. "What would you like?"

"Tomato juice and lemonade," said Trevor, as he pulled a chair in front of the fire and hogged all the heat.

"It's hard work being a farmer," said Henry Bucket from behind the bar. "You're sure you want a cherry in your, um—"

"Cocktail," said Clever Trevor rudely. "I only drink cocktails." He paused. "And I want two cherries and an umbrella."

Henry Bucket stared at him and his big red nose began to glow with anger. "We... don't... have... umbrellas," he said slowly.

Clever Trevor frowned. "Then make it three cherries, a straw and a sugar cube," he said sulkily.

"Coming up," said Henry Bucket in an icy voice.

Clever Trevor spent the whole day at *The Skipping Pig*. He talked about his days as a lifeguard, how important he was, the height of his high chair and what hard work it had all been. Not once did he mention his Great Aunt Emily or Molehills Farm.

"How is the farm?" said Hilda Bucket at last, hoping that Clever Trevor would take the hint and go back to look after his animals. "Your aunt was very proud of her farm. She looked after it all by herself."

"Did she?" said Clever Trevor sounding bored.

"Of course, Snapper was a great help," continued Hilda Bucket. "He was always with her."

"Was he?" said Clever Trevor yawning.

Hilda Bucket looked at her watch. It was past seven o'clock and she knew the cows would need milking.

"How are the cows?" she asked pointedly. "They're a prize-winning herd, you know."

"That right?" said Clever Trevor, staring moodily into his empty glass. "Well, they may have won prizes but they haven't laid a single egg since I've been there. And I like an egg for my breakfast."

Henry and Hilda looked at each other with open mouths. They couldn't believe what they had just heard.

"Nellie's been up to help of course," said Hilda Bucket grimly.

Clever Trevor looked up. "You mean that funny-looking girl with the bobble-hat and glasses?" He leaned forward. "The one that doesn't even wear lipstick?"

"Sounds like my daughter," said Henry Bucket in a low, furious voice.

But Clever Trevor wasn't listening. "She tried to tell me about farming," he sneered. "As if I didn't know anything."

Henry Bucket glared at him. "It seems to me…" he said in a dangerous tone of voice. But he never finished his sentence because the door suddenly blew open and the sound of yapping filled the room. It was a strange, hollow sound and Clever Trevor had heard it the night before. The hairs on the back of his thick neck prickled horribly. Slowly, all the things he thought he had imagined at Molehills Farm crept back into his mind.

BAA! BAA! A flock of sheep thundered through the door! Tables and chairs went flying. Glasses and plates crashed to the floor.

Henry Bucket glared at Clever Trevor.

"These are your sheep!" he roared. He was so furious, his big red nose was flashing on and off like a beacon. "They're hungry! Get out of here and look after them!"

And before Clever Trevor knew what was happening, Hilda Bucket had thrown him into the dark, wet night and driven the sheep out after him.

Chapter Five

Poor Clever Trevor! There he was, pushed on every side by a flock of hungry sheep, with no idea how to get them back to Molehills Farm.

Suddenly, there was a sharp pain in his ankle. Then another and another. Something was biting him! Something with sharp teeth and a cold wet nose!

Clever Trevor looked down, but all he could see were sheep. Then he heard the sound of a dog growling, the same strange, hollow growling he had heard in the sitting room at Molehills Farm and now he knew which dog it was! It was the dog that had disappeared from the painting of his Great Aunt Emily. It was Snapper!

The butterflies in Clever Trevor's stomach grew propellers. Knees knocking, he leapt over the top of the sheep, jumped into the buttercup-yellow car and roared down the muddy track.

The painting was waiting for him when he pushed open the front door. Great Aunt Emily was still there, but now the long, knobbly stick was raised above her head as if she was going to hit somebody with it.

Clever Trevor
couldn't help himself.
He ducked and ran
into the sitting room.
All the windows
were open and the
room was full of
chickens!

Clever Trevor put his hands over his face and threw himself down on a chair.

Squelch! Squelch! Squelch!

He jumped up. A dozen broken eggs lay in a sticky yellow mess on the seat of the chair.

Clever Trevor stared at them in amazement. Chickens? Eggs?

Slowly his mind began to turn things over.

"I thought cows laid eggs," he muttered to himself.

Then another even more extraordinary thought came to him. That must mean that cows not chickens had to be milked. And… Clever Trevor groaned aloud. Maybe sheep didn't scratch for worms after all. He thought of Henry Bucket's angry words: "These are your sheep! They're hungry!" Maybe he was right. Maybe the sheep really were hungry.

For the first time in his life, Clever Trevor felt completely unsure of himself. Maybe he didn't know as much about farming as he thought he did. No wonder Nellie Bucket had given him such a strange look. Perhaps he should borrow Bulging Brian's picture book after all.

A cold, nasty feeling crawled across Clever Trevor's stomach. He began to feel as if he had made a complete fool of himself. It was a brand new feeling, and he didn't like it one little bit.

Grrrr! Grrrr! Clever Trevor spun round and found himself staring straight into the fierce brown eyes of the terrier in the painting.

Clever Trevor tried to push him away with his foot, but his foot went straight through him and out the other side! Before Clever Trevor had time to faint, the terrier grabbed hold of his shiny yellow track suit and dragged him out of the room and down the hall to Great Aunt Emily. Clever Trevor didn't want to look up at her but soon felt the nip of Snapper's sharp teeth in his ankle. He looked up.

Great Aunt Emily's eyes were blazing and her arm was raised with her finger pointing to the yard!

Clever Trevor opened the door and Snapper tugged him across the muddy yard until they came to the rosebush on the other side.

Lying in the mud was the battered dog bowl he had thrown out of the window the day before. It seemed like a lifetime ago.

Clever Trevor bent down and picked it up, then with Snapper growling at his heels he walked back into the house, down the hall, into the sitting room, and put the dog bowl back on the wall above the fireplace.

Brrrrm! Brrrrm!

Bulging Brian's tyres squealed in the yard and for a second Trevor's white face was caught in the headlight of the motorbike. He looked down at his feet. Snapper had disappeared!

Clever Trevor ran into the hall just as Bulging Brian strode in to the house holding a picture book in his hand. Behind him was Nellie Bucket, carrying a box of groceries. This time she didn't give Trevor a strange look. Instead she looked as if she was sorry for him.

"It's hard work being a farmer," said Nellie Bucket kindly. "I brought you these in case you haven't had time to make supper."

"Yeah," said Bulging Brian. "And I brought you my picture book." For a moment, he looked embarrassed. "You can keep it," he added in a gruff voice.

Clever Trevor stared at them both. At first he couldn't think of anything to say.

"Thank you," he mumbled at last, blushing from head to toe. "I don't think I've been very clever." He took a deep breath. "In fact, my real name is Trevor Prat and I think I've been a right one for a long time."

Nellie Bucket grinned at him. "I'll milk the cows. You give the chickens their corn and Brian will feed the sheep," she said. She paused and there was a twinkle in her eye. "Then we'll have supper."

As she spoke, Clever Trevor looked up at the painting of Great Aunt Emily. In one hand she held Snapper and her other hand rested on a long, knobbly stick. The painting was exactly the same as when he had first arrived, except maybe, just maybe, there was a tiny smile on Great Aunt Emily's fierce, bristly face.